Short Stories in Prose and Verse

Henry Lawson

Short Stories in Prose and Verse

BY

Henry Lawson

1894

CONTENTS

PREFACE

This is an attempt to publish, in Australia, a collection of sketches and stories at a time when everything Australian, in the shape of a book, must bear the imprint of a London publishing firm before our critics will condescend to notice it, and before the "reading public" will think it worth its while to buy nearly so many copies as will pay for the mere cost of printing a presentable volume.

The Australian writer, until he gets a "London hearing", is only accepted as an imitator of some recognised English or American author; and, so soon as he shows signs of coming to the front, he is labelled "The Australian Southey", "The Australian Burns", or "The Australian Bret Harte", and, lately, "The Australian Kipling". Thus, no matter how original he may be, he is branded, at the very start, as a plagiarist, and by his own country, which thinks, no doubt, that it is paying him a compliment and encouraging him, while it is really doing him a cruel and an almost irreparable injury.

But, mark! So soon as the Southern writer goes "home" and gets some recognition in England, he is "So-and-So, the well-known Australian author whose work has attracted so much attention in London lately"; and we first hear of him by cable, even though he might have been writing at his best for ten years in Australia.

The same paltry spirit tried to dispose of the greatest of modern short story writers as "The Californian Dickens", but America wasn't built that way—neither was Bret Harte!

To illustrate the above growl: a Sydney daily paper, reviewing the Bulletin's Golden Shanty when the first edition came out, said of my story, "His Father's Mate", that it stood out distinctly as an excellent specimen of that kind of writing which Bret Harte set the world imitating in vain, and, being "full of local colour, it was no unworthy copy of the great master". That critic evidently hadn't studied the "great master" any more than he did my yarn, of Australian goldfield life.

Then he spoke of another story as also having the "Californian flavour". For the other writers I can say that I feel sure they could point out their scenery, and name, or, in some cases, introduce "the reader" to their characters in the flesh. The first seventeen years of my life were spent on the goldfields, and therefore, I didn't need to go back, in imagination, to a time before I was born, and to a country I had never seen, for literary material.

This pamphlet—I can scarcely call it a volume—contains some of my earliest efforts, and they are sufficiently crude and faulty. They have been collected and printed hurriedly, with an eye to Xmas, and without experienced editorial assistance, which last, I begin to think, was sadly necessary.

However, we all hope to do better in future, and I shall have more confidence in my first volume of verse, which will probably be published some time next year. The stories and sketches were originally written for the Bulletin, Worker, Truth, Antipodean Magazine, and the Brisbane Boomerang, which last was one of the many Australian publications which were starved to death because they tried to be original, to be honest, to pay for and encourage Australian literature, and, above all, to be Australian, while the "high average intelligence of the Australians" preferred to patronise thievish imported rags of the "Faked-Bits" order.

"RATS"

"Why, there's two of them, and they're having a fight! Come on. "'

It seemed a strange place for a fight—that hot, lonely, cotton-bush plain. And yet not more than half a mile ahead there were apparently two men struggling together on the track.

The three travellers postponed their smoke-ho and hurried on. They were shearers—a little man and a big man, known respectively as "Sunlight" and "Macquarie, " and a tall, thin, young jackeroo whom they called "Milky. "

"I wonder where the other man sprang from? I didn't see him before, " said Sunlight.

"He muster bin layin' down in the bushes, " said Macquarie. "They're goin' at it proper, too. Come on! Hurry up and see the fun!"

They hurried on.

"It's a funny-lookin' feller, the other feller, " panted Milky. "He don't seem to have no head. Look! he's down—they're both down! They must ha' clinched on the ground. No! they're up an' at it again.... Why, good Lord! I think the other's a woman! "

"My oath! so it is! " yelled Sunlight. "Look! the brute's got her down again! He's kickin' her. Come on, chaps; come on, or he'll do for her!"

They dropped swags, water-bags and all, and raced forward; but presently Sunlight, who had the best eyes, slackened his pace and dropped behind. His mates glanced back at his face, saw a peculiar expression there, looked ahead again, and then dropped into a walk.

They reached the scene of the trouble, and there stood a little withered old man by the track, with his arms folded close up under

1

his chin; he was dressed mostly in calico patches; and half a dozen corks, suspended on bits of string from the brim of his hat, dangled before his bleared optics to scare away the flies. He was scowling malignantly at a stout, dumpy swag which lay in the middle of the track.

"Well, old Rats, what's the trouble? " asked Sunlight.

"Oh, nothing, nothing, " answered the old man, without looking round. "I fell out with my swag, that's all. He knocked me down, but I've settled him. "

"But look here, " said Sunlight, winking at his mates, "we saw you jump on him when he was down. That ain't fair, you know. "

"But you didn't see it all, " cried Rats, getting excited. "He hit me down first! And look here, I'll fight him again for nothing, and you can see fair play. "

They talked awhile; then Sunlight proposed to second the swag, while his mate supported the old man, and after some persuasion, Milky agreed, for the sake of the lark, to act as time-keeper and referee.

Rats entered into the spirit of the thing; he stripped to the waist, and while he was getting ready the travellers pretended to bet on the result.

Macquarie took his place behind the old man, and Sunlight up-ended the swag. Rats shaped and danced round; then he rushed, feinted, ducked, retreated, darted in once more, and suddenly went down like a shot on the broad of his back. No actor could have done it better; he went down from that imaginary blow as if a cannon-ball had struck him in the forehead.

Milky called time, and the old man came up, looking shaky. However, he got in a tremendous blow which knocked the swag into the bushes.

Several rounds followed with varying success.

The men pretended to get more and more excited, and betted freely; and Rats did his best. At last they got tired of the fun, Sunlight let the swag lie after Milky called time, and the jackaroo awarded the fight to Rats. They pretended to hand over the stakes, and then went back for their swags, while the old man put on his shirt.

Then he calmed down, carried his swag to the side of the track, sat down on it and talked rationally about bush matters for a while; but presently he grew silent and began to feel his muscles and smile idiotically.

"Can you len' us a bit o' meat? " said he suddenly.

They spared him half a pound; but he said he didn't want it all, and cut off about an ounce, which he laid on the end of his swag. Then he took the lid off his billy and produced a fishing-line. He baited the hook, threw the line across the track, and waited for a bite. Soon he got deeply interested in the line, jerked it once or twice, and drew it in rapidly. The bait had been rubbed off in the grass. The old man regarded the hook disgustedly.

"Look at that! " he cried. "I had him, only I was in such a hurry. I should ha' played him a little more. "

Next time he was more careful. He drew the line in warily, grabbed an imaginary fish and laid it down on the grass. Sunlight and Co. were greatly interested by this time.

"Wot yer think o' that? " asked Rats. "It weighs thirty pound if it weighs an ounce! Wot yer think o' that for a cod? The hook's half-way down his blessed gullet! "

He caught several cod and a bream while they were there, and invited them to camp and have tea with him. But they wished to reach a certain shed next day, so—after the ancient had borrowed about a pound of meat for bait—they went on, and left him fishing contentedly.

But first Sunlight went down into his pocket and came up with half a crown, which he gave to the old man, along with some tucker. "You'd best push on to the water before dark, old chap, " he said, kindly.

When they turned their heads again, Rats was still fishing but when they looked back for the last time before entering the timber, he was having another row with his swag; and Sunlight reckoned that the trouble arose out of some lies which the swag had been telling about the bigger fish it caught.

WE CALLED HIM "ALLY" FOR SHORT

I don't believe in ghosts; I never did have any sympathy with them, being inclined to regard them as a nuisance and a bore. A ghost generally comes fooling around when you want to go to sleep, and his conversation, if he speaks at all, invariably turns on murders and suicides and other unpleasant things in which you are not interested, and which only disturb your rest. It is no use locking the door against a ghost, for, as is well-known, he can come in through the key hole, and there are cases on record when a ghost has been known to penetrate a solid wall. You cannot kick a ghost out; he is impervious to abuse, and if you throw a boot at him, likely as not it will go right through a new looking-glass worth eighteen shillings.

I remember, about five years ago, I was greatly annoyed by a ghost, while doing a job of fencing in the bush between here and Perth. I was camping in an old house which had been used as a barrack for the convicts or their keepers (I'm not sure which) in the lively old days of the broad arrow. He was a common-looking ghost of a skeleton kind, and was arrayed in what appeared to be the tattered remnants of an old-time convict uniform. He still wore a pair of shadowy manacles, but, being very elastic and unsubstantial and stretching the full length of his stride, he did not seem to notice them at all. He had a kind of Artful Dodger expression about his bare jaw-bones, and in place of the ordinary halo of the ring variety, he wore a shining representation of a broad-arrow which shed a radiance over his skull. He used to come round and wake me about midnight with a confounded rigmarole about a convict who was buried alive in his irons, and whose representative my unwelcome visitor claimed to be. I tried all I knew to discourage him. I told him I wasn't interested and wanted to go to sleep; but his perseverance wore me out at last, and I tried another tack. I listened to his confounded yarn from beginning to end, and sympathised with him, and told him that he, or the individual he represented, had been treated confoundedly badly; and I promised to make a poem about it.

But even then he wasn't satisfied. Nothing would suit him but he must spin his old yarn, and be sympathised with about seven times a week, always choosing the most unbusinesslike hours (between one and three in the morning) for his disclosures.

At last I could stand it no longer. I was getting thin and exhausted from want of sleep, so I determined on a course of action. I had a dog at home, a big black dog with unpleasant eyes, and a chewing-up apparatus that an alligator might have envied. He had a most enterprising appetite, and wasn't afraid of anything on the surface of this earth—or under it—as far as he could burrow. He would gnaw a log to pieces rather than let the 'possum it contained escape him. He was not the sort of dog to stand any nonsense even from a ghost. His full name was Alligator-Desolation (we called him "Ally" for short): and, as I considered that if any person on earth could lay the ghost that annoyed me, that person was Alligator-Desolation, I decided to bring him along.

The next time I journeyed home for rations I brought Alligator-Desolation back with me. On the trip back he killed five kangaroos, sixteen 'possums, four native rats, two native bears, three sheep, a cow and a calf, and another dog that happened by; and before he had been two hours at the hut he had collected enough carcases of indigenous animals to stink a troop out in a week, or to feed all the dogs in Constantinople. I had tea and a smoke while Ally was resting, and about eleven o'clock I lay down in my bunk, dressed as I was, and waited. At about one I heard the usual unearthly noises which accompanied the arrival of my friend the ghost, and Ally went out to investigate. While the dog was gone, the ghost strolled in through the door of the end room, apparently unconscious of his danger. He glided straight up to the side of my bunk, took his accustomed seat on a gin-case, and commenced in a doleful voice to pitch his confounded old yarn again; but he hadn't uttered half-a-dozen ghostly words when Alligator-Desolation came in through the side door.

The ghost caught sight of Ally before the latter saw him, and made for the window. Ally wasn't far behind; he made a grab at the ghost's nether garments, but they gave way easily, being of a ghostly material. Then Ally leapt out through the window and chased the ghost three times round the house, and then the latter came in through an opening in the wall where a slab had fallen out. Being of an easily compressible constitution he came through, of course, with the facility peculiar to his kind, but the crack was narrow and the dog stuck fast. His ghostship made the best of his opportunity, and, approaching my bed, hurriedly endeavoured to continue his story, as though his ghostly existence depended on it. But his utterances were drowned by the language of Alligator, whose canine oaths were simply terrific. At last, collecting all his energy for one mighty effort, Alligator came through, bringing down the slabs on each side of him.

He made for the ghost at once, and the ghost made for the window. This time Alligator made a grab for the spectre's ankle, and his teeth came together with a crash that threatened their destruction. Ally must have been greatly astonished and disgusted, because he so seldom missed anything he reached for. But he wasn't the kind of dog to give up. He leapt through the window, and, after a race round the hut, lasting some minutes, the ghost gave it up, and made for the scrub. Seeing the retreat through a crack in the slabs, I immediately rose, went outside and mounted my horse, which I had kept ready saddled in case of emergency. I followed the chase for about five miles, and at last reached a mound under some trees, which looked like an old grave. Down through this mound the ghost dived.

Alligator-Desolation immediately commenced to dig, and made two feet in no time. It appeared that a wombat had selected the grave as a suitable site for the opening of his burrow and after having sunk about three feet, was resting from his labours. There was a short and angry interview between Alligator and the wombat, during which the latter expired, and then Ally continued his work of excavation. After sinking two feet deeper he dragged out what appeared to be the leg-bone of a human being, attached to which was a pair of heavy leg-irons, such as were used in the old convict days. Ally went down the hole again, but presently he paused in his digging operations, and I heard a noise like a row in the infernal regions. Then a thin shadowy form issued from the grave and made off through the scrub with the dog in pursuit.

My horse was knocked up, so I left the chase to Alligator and returned home to await developments. Ally came back about three days later with his hair badly singed and smelling strongly of brimstone. I have no doubt that he chased the ghost to the infernal regions and perhaps had an interview with Cerberus at the gate, or the boss himself; but the dog's tail was well up and a satisfied grin oozed from the roots of every fang, and by the same tokens I concluded that the other party, whoever he was, had got fatally left.

I haven't seen the ghost since.

BUSH CATS

"Domestic cats" we mean—the descendants of cats who came from the northern world during the last hundred odd years. We do not know the name of the vessel in which the first Thomas and his Maria came out to Australia, but we suppose that it was one of the ships of the First Fleet. Most likely Maria had kittens on the voyage —two lots, perhaps—the majority of which were buried at sea; and no doubt the disembarkation caused her much maternal anxiety.

* * * * *

The feline race has not altered much in Australia, from a physical point of view—not yet. The rabbit has developed into something like a cross between a kangaroo and a possum, but the bush has not begun to develop the common cat. She is just as sedate and motherly as the mummy cats of Egypt were, but she takes longer strolls of nights, climbs gum-trees instead of roofs, and hunts stranger vermin than ever came under the observation of her northern ancestors. Her views have widened. She is mostly thinner than the English farm cat—which is, they say, on account of eating lizards.

English rats and English mice—we say "English" because everything which isn't Australian in Australia, IS English (or British)—English rats and English mice are either rare or non-existent in the bush; but the hut cat has a wider range for game. She is always dragging in things which are unknown in the halls of zoology; ugly, loathsome, crawling abortions which have not been classified yet—and perhaps could not be.

The Australian zoologist ought to rake up some more dead languages, and then go Out Back with a few bush cats.

The Australian bush cat has a nasty, unpleasant habit of dragging a long, wriggling, horrid, black snake—she seems to prefer black snakes—into a room where there are ladies, proudly laying it down in a conspicuous place (usually in front of the exit), and then looking up for approbation. She wonders, perhaps, why the visitors are in such a hurry to leave.

Pussy doesn't approve of live snakes round the place, especially if she has kittens; and if she finds a snake in the vicinity of her progeny—well, it is bad for that particular serpent.

This brings recollections of a neighbour's cat who went out in the scrub, one midsummer's day, and found a brown snake. Her name —the cat's name—was Mary Ann. She got hold of the snake all right, just within an inch of its head; but it got the rest of its length wound round her body and squeezed about eight lives out of her. She had the presence of mind to keep her hold; but it struck her that she was in a fix, and that if she wanted to save her ninth life, it wouldn't be a bad idea to go home for help. So she started home, snake and all.

The family were at dinner when Mary Ann came in, and, although she stood on an open part of the floor, no one noticed her for a while. She couldn't ask for help, for her mouth was too full of snake. By-and-bye one of the girls glanced round, and then went over the table, with a shriek, and out of the back door. The room was cleared very quickly. The eldest boy got a long-handled shovel, and in another second would have killed more cat than snake; but his father interfered. The father was a shearer, and Mary Ann was a favourite cat with him. He got a pair of shears from the shelf and deftly shore off the snake's head, and one side of Mary Ann's whiskers. She didn't think it safe to let go yet. She kept her teeth in the neck until the selector snipped the rest of the snake off her. The bits were carried out on a shovel to die at sundown. Mary Ann had a good drink of milk, and then got her tongue out and licked herself back into the proper shape for a cat; after which she went out to look for that snake's mate. She found it, too, and dragged it home the same evening.

Cats will kill rabbits and drag them home. We knew a fossicker whose cat used to bring him a bunny nearly every night. The fossicker had rabbits for breakfast until he got sick of them, and then he used to swap them with a butcher for meat. The cat was named

Ingersoll, which indicates his sex and gives an inkling to his master's religious and political opinions. Ingersoll used to prospect round in the gloaming until he found some rabbit holes which showed encouraging indications. He would shepherd one hole for an hour or so every evening until he found it was a duffer, or worked it out; then he would shift to another. One day he prospected a big hollow log with a lot of holes in it, and more going down underneath. The indications were very good, but Ingersoll had no luck. The game had too many ways of getting out and in. He found that he could not work that claim by himself, so he floated it into a company. He persuaded several cats from a neighbouring selection to take shares, and they watched the holes together, or in turns—they worked shifts. The dividends more than realised even their wildest expectations, for each cat took home at least one rabbit every night for a week.

A selector started a vegetable garden about the time when rabbits were beginning to get troublesome up country. The hare had not shown itself yet. The farmer kept quite a regiment of cats to protect his garden—and they protected it. He would shut the cats up all day with nothing to eat, and let them out about sundown; then they would mooch off to the turnip patch like farm-labourers going to work. They would drag the rabbits home to the back door, and sit there and watch them until the farmer opened the door and served out the ration of milk. Then the cats would turn in. He nearly always found a semi-circle of dead rabbits and watchful cats round the door in the morning. They sold the product of their labour direct to the farmer for milk. It didn't matter if one cat had been unlucky —had not got a rabbit—each had an equal share in the general result. They were true socialists, those cats.

One of those cats was a mighty big Tom, named Jack. He was death on rabbits; he would work hard all night, laying for them and dragging them home. Some weeks he would graft every night, and at other times every other night, but he was generally pretty regular. When he reckoned he had done an extra night's work, he would take the next night off and go three miles to the nearest neighbour's to see his Maria and take her out for a stroll. Well, one evening Jack went into the garden and chose a place where there was good cover, and lay low. He was a bit earlier than usual, so he thought he would have a doze till rabbit time. By-and-bye he heard a noise, and slowly, cautiously opening one eye, he saw two big ears sticking out of the leaves in front of him. He judged that it was an extra big bunny, so he put some extra style into his manoeuvres. In about five minutes he made his spring. He must have thought (if cats think) that it was a whopping, old-man rabbit, for it was a pioneer hare—not an ordinary English hare, but one of those great coarse, lanky things which the bush is breeding. The selector was attracted by an unusual commotion and a cloud of dust among his cabbages, and came along with his gun in time to witness the fight. First Jack would drag the hare, and then the hare would drag Jack; sometimes they would be down together, and then Jack would use his hind claws with effect; finally he got his teeth in the right place, and triumphed. Then he started to drag the corpse home, but he had to give it best and ask his master to lend a hand. The selector took up the hare, and Jack followed home, much to the family's surprise. He did not go back to work that night; he took a spell. He had a drink of milk, licked the dust off himself, washed it down with another drink, and sat in front of the fire and thought for a goodish while. Then he got up, walked over to the corner where the hare was lying, had a good look at it, came back to the fire, sat down again, and thought hard. He was still thinking when the family retired.

A NARROW ESCAPE

I suppose the reader has experienced or heard of hair-breadth escapes, the memory of which has caused his own hair to stand on end; yet, when he has read the following untruthful story, he will be ready to exclaim in a tone of intense conviction that truth is indeed stranger than fiction.

A few years ago I was travelling with a prospecting party in some place, and one morning I awoke and found my horse gone.

Without disturbing my companions, I took a bridle and started to follow up the horse's tracks across the sand.

The horse must have broken loose some time in the night, for I followed his tracks a good distance until they disappeared in a grass patch. I wandered about for some time in a vain endeavour to pick up the trail, and ended up by getting lost myself.

The morning passed away, and I was still wandering hopefully, when, about noon, I descried three dark figures on the horizon of the plain. I soon saw that they were blacks, and that they were coming in my direction. As they advanced nearer I saw that one was armed with a nulla nulla or club, whilst the other two carried spears which they brandished in an unpleasant manner. I knew there was not a moment to lose if I wished to save my life (which I did) so I started to run. It was an awful race. I felt my underclothing sticking to my body with the perspiration, and my braces and bootlaces gently giving out.

I kept on under the broiling heat, with the blacks steadily gaining in the rear, until at last I felt that I could run no longer. My time was come. I fell on the glistening sand and prayed for a sudden and comparatively painless death.

The blacks came up and surrounded me, and I saw in their looks that I could not expect mercy at their hands. The memories of my life went through my brain like a flash of lightning, or rather like flashes of lightning. The two blacks, who were armed with spears, raised their weapons to a horizontal position and aimed the points at my heart.

They swayed the spears backward and forward several times to gain momentum. The suspense was very trying indeed. I drew a long breath and attempted to close my eyes; but just as they swung their spears back for a final and fatal thrust the blackfellow who carried the club, and who had up to this moment stood perfectly still and silent, suddenly raised his weapon and brought it down on my head with a sickening crash, and I fell at his feet a ghastly corpse.

JOHNSON, ALIAS CROW

Where the seasons are divided and the bush begins to change, and the links are rather broken in the Great Dividing Range; where the atmosphere is hazy underneath the summer sky, lies the little town of Eton, rather westward of Mackay. Near the township, in the graveyard, where the dead of Eton go, lies the body of a sinner known as "Johnson alias Crow". He was sixty-four was Johnson, and in other days, lang syne, was apprenticed to a ship-wright in the land across the Rhine; but, whatever were his prospects in the days of long ago, things went very bad with Johnson—Heinrich Johnson (alias Crow). He, at Eton—where he drifted in his age, a stranded wreck—got three pounds by false pretences, in connection with a cheque. But he didn't long enjoy it, the police soon got to know; and the lockup closed on Johnson, lonely Johnson alias Crow. Friday night, and Crow retired, feeling, as he said, unwell; and the warder heard the falling of a body in the cell. Going in, the warder saw him bent with pain and crouching low—Death had laid his hand on Johnson, Heinrich Johnson, alias Crow. Then the constable bent o'er him—asked him where he felt the pain. Johnson only said, "I'm dying"—and he never spoke again. They had waited for a witness, and the local people say Johnson's trial would have ended on that very Saturday; but he took his case for judgment where our cases all must go, and the higher court is trying Heinrich Johnson (alias Crow).

THE FIRE AT ROSS'S FARM

The squatter saw his pastures wide
 Decrease, as one by one
The farmers moving to the west
 Selected on his run;
Selectors took the water up
 And all the black soil round;
The best grass-land the squatter had
 Was spoilt by Ross's Ground.

Now many schemes to shift old Ross
 Had racked the squatter's brains,
But Sandy had the stubborn blood
 Of Scotland in his veins;
He held the land and fenced it in,
 He cleared and ploughed the soil,
And year by year a richer crop
 Repaid him for his toil.

Between the homes for many years
 The devil left his tracks:
The squatter pounded Ross's stock,
 And Sandy pounded Black's.
A well upon the lower run
 Was filled with earth and logs,
And Black laid baits about the farm
 To poison Ross's dogs.

It was, indeed, a deadly feud
 Of class and creed and race;
But, yet, there was a Romeo
 And a Juliet in the case;
And more than once across the flats,
 Beneath the Southern Cross,
Young Robert Black was seen to ride
 With pretty Jenny Ross.

One Christmas time, when months of drought
  Had parched the western creeks,
The bush-fires started in the north
  And travelled south for weeks.
At night along the river-side
  The scene was grand and strange—
The hill-fires looked like lighted streets
  Of cities in the range.

The cattle-tracks between the trees
  Were like long dusky aisles,
And on a sudden breeze the fire
  Would sweep along for miles;
Like sounds of distant musketry
  It crackled through the brakes,
And o'er the flat of silver grass
  It hissed like angry snakes.

It leapt across the flowing streams
  And raced o'er pastures broad;
It climbed the trees and lit the boughs
  And through the scrubs it roared.
The bees fell stifled in the smoke
  Or perished in their hives,
And with the stock the kangaroos
  Went flying for their lives.

The sun had set on Christmas Eve,
  When, through the scrub-lands wide,
Young Robert Black came riding home
  As only natives ride.
He galloped to the homestead door
  And gave the first alarm:
'The fire is past the granite spur,
  'And close to Ross's farm.'

'Now, father, send the men at once,
  They won't be wanted here;

Poor Ross's wheat is all he has
 To pull him through the year.'
'Then let it burn,' the squatter said;
 'I'd like to see it done —
I'd bless the fire if it would clear
 Selectors from the run.

'Go if you will,' the squatter said,
 'You shall not take the men —
Go out and join your precious friends,
 And don't come here again.'
'I won't come back,' young Robert cried,
 And, reckless in his ire,
He sharply turned his horse's head
 And galloped towards the fire.

And there, for three long weary hours,
 Half-blind with smoke and heat,
Old Ross and Robert fought the flames
 That neared the ripened wheat.
The farmer's hand was nerved by fears
 Of danger and of loss;
And Robert fought the stubborn foe
 For the love of Jenny Ross.

But serpent-like the curves and lines
 Slipped past them, and between,
Until they reached the bound'ry where
 The old coach-road had been.
'The track is now our only hope,
 There we must stand,' cried Ross,
'For nought on earth can stop the fire
 If once it gets across.'

Then came a cruel gust of wind,
 And, with a fiendish rush,
The flames leapt o'er the narrow path
 And lit the fence of brush.

'The crop must burn!' the farmer cried,
 'We cannot save it now,'
And down upon the blackened ground
 He dashed the ragged bough.

But wildly, in a rush of hope,
 His heart began to beat,
For o'er the crackling fire he heard
 The sound of horses' feet.
'Here's help at last,' young Robert cried,
 And even as he spoke
The squatter with a dozen men
 Came racing through the smoke.

Down on the ground the stockmen jumped
 And bared each brawny arm,
They tore green branches from the trees
 And fought for Ross's farm;
And when before the gallant band
 The beaten flames gave way,
Two grimy hands in friendship joined —
 And it was Christmas Day.

THE DROVER'S WIFE

The two-roomed house is built of round timber, slabs, and stringy-bark, and floored with split slabs. A big bark kitchen standing at one end is larger than the house itself, veranda included.

Bush all round—bush with no horizon, for the country is flat. No ranges in the distance. The bush consists of stunted, rotten native apple-trees. No undergrowth. Nothing to relieve the eye save the darker green of a few she-oaks which are sighing above the narrow, almost waterless creek. Nineteen miles to the nearest sign of civilization—a shanty on the main road.

The drover, an ex-squatter, is away with sheep. His wife and children are left here alone.

Four ragged, dried-up-looking children are playing about the house. Suddenly one of them yells: "Snake! Mother, here's a snake! "

The gaunt, sun-browned bushwoman dashes from the kitchen, snatches her baby from the ground, holds it on her left hip, and reaches for a stick.

"Where is it? "

"Here! gone into the wood-heap! " yells the eldest boy—a sharp-faced urchin of eleven. "Stop there, mother! I'll have him. Stand back! I'll have the beggar! "

"Tommy, come here, or you'll be bit. Come here at once when I tell you, you little wretch! "

The youngster comes reluctantly, carrying a stick bigger than himself. Then he yells, triumphantly:

"There it goes—under the house! " and darts away with club uplifted. At the same time the big, black, yellow-eyed dog-of-all-breeds, who has shown the wildest interest in the proceedings, breaks his chain and rushes after that snake. He is a moment late, however, and his nose reaches the crack in the slabs just as the end of its tail disappears. Almost at the same moment the boy's club comes down and skins the aforesaid nose. Alligator takes small notice of this, and proceeds to undermine the building; but he is subdued after a struggle and chained up. They cannot afford to lose him.

The drover's wife makes the children stand together near the dog-house while she watches for the snake. She gets two small dishes of milk and sets them down near the wall to tempt it to come out; but an hour goes by and it does not show itself.

It is near sunset, and a thunderstorm is coming. The children must be brought inside. She will not take them into the house, for she knows the snake is there, and may at any moment come up through a crack in the rough slab floor; so she carries several armfuls of firewood into the kitchen, and then takes the children there. The kitchen has no floor—or, rather, an earthen one—called a "ground floor" in this part of the bush. There is a large, roughly-made table in the centre of the place. She brings the children in, and makes them get on this table. They are two boys and two girls—mere babies. She gives them some supper, and then, before it gets dark, she goes into the house, and snatches up some pillows and bedclothes—expecting to see or lay her hand on the snake any minute. She makes a bed on the kitchen table for the children, and sits down beside it to watch all night.

She has an eye on the corner, and a green sapling club laid in readiness on the dresser by her side; also her sewing basket and a copy of the Young Ladies' Journal. She has brought the dog into the room.

Tommy turns in, under protest, but says he'll lie awake all night and smash that blinded snake.

His mother asks him how many times she has told him not to swear.

He has his club with him under the bedclothes, and Jacky protests:

"Mummy! Tommy's skinnin' me alive wif his club. Make him take it out. "

Tommy: "Shet up, you little —-! D'yer want to be bit with the snake?"

Jacky shuts up.

"If yer bit, " says Tommy, after a pause, "you'll swell up, an' smell, an' turn red an' green an' blue all over till yer bust. Won't he, mother? "

"Now then, don't frighten the child. Go to sleep, " she says.

The two younger children go to sleep, and now and then Jacky complains of being "skeezed. " More room is made for him. Presently Tommy says: "Mother! listen to them (adjective) little possums. I'd like to screw their blanky necks. "

And Jacky protests drowsily.

"But they don't hurt us, the little blanks! ".

Mother: "There, I told you you'd teach Jacky to swear. " But the remark makes her smile. Jacky goes to sleep. Presently Tommy asks:

"Mother! Do you think they'll ever extricate the (adjective) kangaroo? "

"Lord! How am I to know, child? Go to sleep. "

"Will you wake me if the snake comes out? "

"Yes. Go to sleep. "

Near midnight. The children are all asleep and she sits there still, sewing and reading by turns. From time to time she glances round the floor and wall-plate, and, whenever she hears a noise, she reaches for the stick. The thunderstorm comes on, and the wind, rushing through the cracks in the slab wall, threatens to blow out her candle. She places it on a sheltered part of the dresser and fixes up a newspaper to protect it. At every flash of lightning, the cracks between the slabs gleam like polished silver. The thunder rolls, and the rain comes down in torrents.

Alligator lies at full length on the floor, with his eyes turned towards the partition. She knows by this that the snake is there. There are large cracks in that wall opening under the floor of the dwelling-house.

She is not a coward, but recent events have shaken her nerves. A little son of her brother-in-law was lately bitten by a snake, and died. Besides, she has not heard from her husband for six months, and is anxious about him.

He was a drover, and started squatting here when they were married. The drought of 18—ruined him. He had to sacrifice the remnant of his flock and go droving again. He intends to move his family into the nearest town when he comes back, and, in the meantime, his brother, who keeps a shanty on the main road, comes over about once a month with provisions. The wife has still a couple of cows, one horse, and a few sheep. The brother-in-law kills one of the latter occasionally, gives her what she needs of it, and takes the rest in return for other provisions. She is used to being left alone. She once lived like this for eighteen months. As a girl she built the usual castles in the air; but all her girlish hopes and aspirations have long been dead. She finds all the excitement and recreation she needs in the Young Ladies' Journal, and Heaven help her! takes a pleasure in the fashion-plates.

Her husband is an Australian, and so is she. He is careless, but a good enough husband. If he had the means he would take her to the city and keep her there like a princess. They are used to being apart, or at least she is. "No use fretting, " she says. He may forget sometimes that he is married; but if he has a good cheque when he comes back he will give most of it to her. When he had money he took her to the city several times—hired a railway sleeping compartment, and put up at the best hotels. He also bought her a buggy, but they had to sacrifice that along with the rest.

The last two children were born in the bush—one while her husband was bringing a drunken doctor, by force, to attend to her. She was alone on this occasion, and very weak. She had been ill with a fever. She prayed to God to send her assistance. God sent Black Mary—the "whitest" gin in all the land. Or, at least, God sent King Jimmy first, and he sent Black Mary. He put his black face round the door post, took in the situation at a glance, and said cheerfully: "All right, missus—I bring my old woman, she down alonga creek. "

One of the children died while she was here alone. She rode nineteen miles for assistance, carrying the dead child.

It must be near one or two o'clock. The fire is burning low. Alligator lies with his head resting on his paws, and watches the wall. He is not a very beautiful dog, and the light shows numerous old wounds where the hair will not grow. He is afraid of nothing on the face of the earth or under it. He will tackle a bullock as readily as he will tackle a flea. He hates all other dogs—except kangaroo-dogs—and has a marked dislike to friends or relations of the family. They seldom call, however. He sometimes makes friends with strangers. He hates snakes and has killed many, but he will be bitten some day and die; most snake-dogs end that way.

Now and then the bushwoman lays down her work and watches, and listens, and thinks. She thinks of things in her own life, for there is little else to think about.

The rain will make the grass grow, and this reminds her how she fought a bush-fire once while her husband was away. The grass was long, and very dry, and the fire threatened to burn her out. She put on an old pair of her husband's trousers and beat out the flames with a green bough, till great drops of sooty perspiration stood out on her forehead and ran in streaks down her blackened arms. The sight of his mother in trousers greatly amused Tommy, who worked like a little hero by her side, but the terrified baby howled lustily for his "mummy. " The fire would have mastered her but for four excited bushmen who arrived in the nick of time. It was a mixed-up affair all round; when she went to take up the baby he screamed and struggled convulsively, thinking it was a "blackman; " and Alligator, trusting more to the child's sense than his own instinct, charged furiously, and (being old and slightly deaf) did not in his excitement at first recognize his mistress's voice, but continued to hang on to the moleskins until choked off by Tommy with a saddle-strap. The dog's sorrow for his blunder, and his anxiety to let it be known that it was all a mistake, was as evident as his ragged tail and a twelve-inch grin could make it. It was a glorious time for the boys; a day to look back to, and talk about, and laugh over for many years.

She thinks how she fought a flood during her husband's absence. She stood for hours in the drenching downpour, and dug an overflow gutter to save the dam across the creek. But she could not save it. There are things that a bushwoman can not do. Next morning the dam was broken, and her heart was nearly broken too, for she thought how her husband would feel when he came home and saw the result of years of labour swept away. She cried then.

She also fought the pleuro-pneumonia—dosed and bled the few remaining cattle, and wept again when her two best cows died.

Again, she fought a mad bullock that besieged the house for a day. She made bullets and fired at him through cracks in the slabs with an old shot-gun. He was dead in the morning. She skinned him and got seventeen-and-sixpence for the hide.

She also fights the crows and eagles that have designs on her chickens. Her plan of campaign is very original. The children cry "Crows, mother! " and she rushes out and aims a broomstick at the birds as though it were a gun, and says "Bung! " The crows leave in a hurry; they are cunning, but a woman's cunning is greater.

Occasionally a bushman in the horrors, or a villainous-looking sundowner, comes and nearly scares the life out of her. She generally tells the suspicious-looking stranger that her husband and two sons are at work below the dam, or over at the yard, for he always cunningly inquires for the boss.

Only last week a gallows-faced swagman—having satisfied himself that there were no men on the place—threw his swag down on the veranda, and demanded tucker. She gave him something to eat; then he expressed his intention of staying for the night. It was sundown then. She got a batten from the sofa, loosened the dog, and confronted the stranger, holding the batten in one hand and the dog's collar with the other. "Now you go! " she said. He looked at her and at the dog, said "All right, mum, " in a cringing tone, and left. She was a determined-looking woman, and Alligator's yellow eyes glared unpleasantly—besides, the dog's chawing-up apparatus greatly resembled that of the reptile he was named after.

She has few pleasures to think of as she sits here alone by the fire, on guard against a snake. All days are much the same to her; but on Sunday afternoon she dresses herself, tidies the children, smartens up baby, and goes for a lonely walk along the bush-track, pushing an old perambulator in front of her. She does this every Sunday. She takes as much care to make herself and the children look smart as she would if she were going to do the block in the city. There is nothing to see, however, and not a soul to meet. You might walk for twenty miles along this track without being able to fix a point in your mind, unless you are a bushman. This is because of the everlasting, maddening sameness of the stunted trees—that monotony which makes a man long to break away and travel as far as trains can go, and sail as far as ship can sail—and farther.

But this bushwoman is used to the loneliness of it. As a girl-wife she hated it, but now she would feel strange away from it.

She is glad when her husband returns, but she does not gush or make a fuss about it. She gets him something good to eat, and tidies up the children.

She seems contented with her lot. She loves her children, but has no time to show it. She seems harsh to them. Her surroundings are not favourable to the development of the "womanly" or sentimental side of nature.

It must be near morning now; but the clock is in the dwellinghouse. Her candle is nearly done; she forgot that she was out of candles. Some more wood must be got to keep the fire up, and so she shuts the dog inside and hurries round to the woodheap. The rain has cleared off. She seizes a stick, pulls it out, and—crash! the whole pile collapses.

Yesterday she bargained with a stray blackfellow to bring her some wood, and while he was at work she went in search of a missing cow. She was absent an hour or so, and the native black made good use of his time. On her return she was so astonished to see a good heap of wood by the chimney, that she gave him an extra fig of tobacco, and praised him for not being lazy. He thanked her, and left with head erect and chest well out. He was the last of his tribe and a King; but he had built that wood-heap hollow.

She is hurt now, and tears spring to her eyes as she sits down again by the table. She takes up a handkerchief to wipe the tears away, but pokes her eyes with her bare fingers instead. The handkerchief is full of holes, and she finds that she has put her thumb through one, and her forefinger through another.

This makes her laugh, to the surprise of the dog. She has a keen, very keen, sense of the ridiculous; and some time or other she will amuse bushmen with the story.

She had been amused before like that. One day she sat down "to have a good cry, " as she said—and the old cat rubbed against her dress and "cried too. " Then she had to laugh.

It must be near daylight now. The room is very close and hot because of the fire. Alligator still watches the wall from time to time. Suddenly he becomes greatly interested; he draws himself a few inches nearer the partition, and a thrill runs through his body. The hair on the back of his neck begins to bristle, and the battle-light is in his yellow eyes. She knows what this means, and lays her hand on the stick. The lower end of one of the partition slabs has a large crack on both sides. An evil pair of small, bright bead-like eyes glisten at one of these holes. The snake—a black one—comes slowly out, about a foot, and moves its head up and down. The dog lies still, and the woman sits as one fascinated. The snake comes out a foot farther. She lifts her stick, and the reptile, as though suddenly aware of danger, sticks his head in through the crack on the other side of the slab, and hurries to get his tail round after him. Alligator springs, and his jaws come together with a snap. He misses, for his nose is large, and the snake's body close down in the angle formed by the slabs and the floor. He snaps again as the tail comes round. He has the snake now, and tugs it out eighteen inches. Thud, thud comes the woman's club on the ground. Alligator pulls again. Thud, thud. Alligator gives another pull and he has the snake out—a black brute, five feet long. The head rises to dart about, but the dog has the enemy close to the neck. He is a big, heavy dog, but quick as a terrier. He shakes the snake as though he felt the original curse in common with mankind. The eldest boy wakes up, seizes his stick, and tries to get out of bed, but his mother forces him back with a grip of iron. Thud, thud—the snake's back is broken in several places. Thud, thud—its head is crushed, and Alligator's nose skinned again.

She lifts the mangled reptile on the point of her stick, carries it to the fire, and throws it in; then piles on the wood and watches the snake burn. The boy and dog watch too. She lays her hand on the dog's head, and all the fierce, angry light dies out of his yellow eyes. The younger children are quieted, and presently go to sleep. The dirty-legged boy stands for a moment in his shirt, watching the fire. Presently he looks up at her, sees the tears in her eyes, and, throwing his arms round her neck exclaims:

"Mother, I won't never go drovin'; blarst me if I do! " And she hugs him to her worn-out breast and kisses him; and they sit thus together while the sickly daylight breaks over the bush.

THE UNION BURIES ITS DEAD

While out boating one Sunday afternoon on a billabong across the river, we saw a young man on horseback driving some horses along the bank. He said it was a fine day, and asked if the Water was deep there. The joker of our party said it was deep enough to drown him, and he laughed and rode farther up. We didn't take-much notice of him.

Next day a funeral gathered at a corner pub and asked each other in to have a drink while waiting for the hearse. They passed away some of the time dancing jigs to a piano in the bar parlour. They passed away the rest of the time skylarking and fighting.

The defunct was a young Union labourer, about twenty-five, who had been drowned the previous day while trying to swim some horses across a billabong of the Darling.

He was almost a stranger in town, and the fact of his having been a Union man accounted for the funeral. The police found some Union papers in his swag, and called at the General Labourers' Union Office for information about him. That's how we knew. The secretary had very little information to give. The departed was a "Roman, " and the majority of the town were otherwise—but Unionism is stronger than creed. Liquor, however, is stronger than Unionism; and, when the hearse presently arrived, more than two-thirds of the funeral were unable to follow.

The procession numbered fifteen, fourteen souls following the broken shell of a soul. Perhaps not one of the fourteen possessed a soul any more than the corpse did—but that doesn't matter.

Four or five of the funeral, who were boarders at the pub, borrowed a trap which the landlord used to carry passengers to and from the railway station. They were strangers to us who were on foot, and we to them. We were all strangers to the corpse.

A horseman, who looked like a drover just returned from a big trip, dropped into our dusty wake and followed us a few hundred yards, dragging his packhorse behind him, but a friend made wild and demonstrative signals from a hotel veranda—hooking at the air in front with his right hand and jobbing his left thumb over his shoulder in the direction of the bar—so the drover hauled off and didn't catch up to us any more. He was a stranger to the entire show.

We walked in twos. There were three twos. It was very hot and dusty; the heat rushed in fierce dazzling rays across every iron roof and light-coloured wall that was turned to the sun. One or two pubs closed respectfully until we got past. They closed their bar doors and the patrons went in and out through some side or back entrance for a few minutes. Bushmen seldom grumble at an inconvenience of this sort, when it is caused by a funeral. They have too much respect for the dead.

On the way to the cemetery we passed three shearers sitting on the shady side of a fence. One was drunk—very drunk. The other two covered their right ears with their hats, out of respect for the departed—whoever he might have been—and one of them kicked the drunk and muttered something to him.

He straightened himself up, stared, and reached helplessly for his hat, which he shoved half off and then on again. Then he made a great effort to pull himself together—and succeeded. He stood up, braced his back against the fence, knocked off his hat, and remorsefully placed his foot on it—to keep it off his head till the funeral passed.

A tall, sentimental drover, who walked by my side, cynically quoted Byronic verses suitable to the occasion—to death—and asked with pathetic humour whether we thought the dead man's ticket would be recognized "over yonder. " It was a G. L.U. ticket, and the general opinion was that it would be recognized.

Presently my friend said:

"You remember when we were in the boat yesterday, we saw a man driving some horses along the bank? "

"Yes. "

He nodded at the hearse and said "Well, that's him. "

I thought awhile.

"I didn't take any particular notice of him, " I said. "He said something, didn't he? "

"Yes; said it was a fine day. You'd have taken more notice if you'd known that he was doomed to die in the hour, and that those were the last words he would say to any man in this world. "

"To be sure, " said a full voice from the rear. "If ye'd known that, ye'd have prolonged the conversation. "

We plodded on across the railway line and along the hot, dusty road which ran to the cemetery, some of us talking about the accident, and lying about the narrow escapes we had had ourselves. Presently someone said:

"There's the Devil. "

I looked up and saw a priest standing in the shade of the tree by the cemetery gate.

The hearse was drawn up and the tail-boards were opened. The funeral extinguished its right ear with its hat as four men lifted the coffin out and laid it over the grave. The priest—a pale, quiet young fellow—stood under the shade of a sapling which grew at the head of the grave. He took off his hat, dropped it carelessly on the ground, and proceeded to business. I noticed that one or two heathens winced slightly when the holy water was sprinkled on the coffin. The drops quickly evaporated, and the little round black spots they left were soon dusted over; but the spots showed, by contrast, the cheapness and shabbiness of the cloth with which the coffin was covered. It seemed black before; now it looked a dusky grey.

Just here man's ignorance and vanity made a farce of the funeral. A big, bull-necked publican, with heavy, blotchy features, and a supremely ignorant expression, picked up the priest's straw hat and held it about two inches over the head of his reverence during the whole of the service. The father, be it remembered, was standing in the shade. A few shoved their hats on and off uneasily, struggling between their disgust far the living and their respect for the dead. The hat had a conical crown and a brim sloping down all round like a sunshade, and the publican held it with his great red claw spread over the crown. To do the priest justice, perhaps he didn't notice the incident. A stage priest or parson in the same position might have said, "Put the hat down, my friend; is not the memory of our departed brother worth more than my complexion? " A wattle-bark layman might have expressed himself in stronger language, none the less to the point. But my priest seemed unconscious of what was going on. Besides, the publican was a great and important pillar of the church. He couldn't, as an ignorant and conceited ass, lose such a good opportunity of asserting his faithfulness and importance to his church.

The grave looked very narrow under the coffin, and I drew a breath of relief when the box slid easily down. I saw a coffin get stuck once, at Rookwood, and it had to be yanked out with difficulty, and laid on the sods at the feet of the heart-broken relations, who howled dismally while the grave-diggers widened the hole. But they don't cut contracts so fine in the West. Our grave-digger was not altogether bowelless, and, out of respect for that human quality described as "feelin's, " he scraped up some light and dusty soil and threw it down to deaden the fall of the clay lumps on the coffin. He also tried to steer the first few shovelfuls gently down against the end of the grave with the back of the shovel turned outwards, but the hard dry Darling River clods rebounded and knocked all the same. It didn't matter much—nothing does. The fall of lumps of clay on a stranger's coffin doesn't sound any different from the fall of the same things on an ordinary wooden box—at least I didn't notice anything awesome or unusual in the sound; but, perhaps, one of us—the most sensitive—might have been impressed by being reminded of a burial of long ago, when the thump of every sod jolted his heart.

I have left out the wattle—because it wasn't there. I have also neglected to mention the heart-broken old mate, with his grizzled head bowed and great pearly drops streaming down his rugged cheeks. He was absent—he was probably "Out Back. " For similar reasons I have omitted reference to the suspicious moisture in the eyes of a bearded bush ruffian named Bill. Bill failed to turn up, and the only moisture was that which was induced by the heat. I have left out the "sad Australian sunset" because the sun was not going down at the time. The burial took place exactly at midday.

The dead bushman's name was Jim, apparently; but they found no portraits, nor locks of hair, nor any love letters, nor anything of that kind in his swag—not even a reference to his mother; only some papers relating to Union matters. Most of us didn't know the name till we saw it on the coffin; we knew him as "that poor chap that got drowned yesterday. "

"So his name's James Tyson, " said my drover acquaintance, looking at the plate.

"Why! Didn't you know that before? " I asked.

"No; but I knew he was a Union man. "

It turned out, afterwards, that J. T. wasn't his real name—only "the name he went by. " Anyhow he was buried by it, and most of the "Great Australian Dailies" have mentioned in their brevity columns that a young man named James John Tyson was drowned in a billabong of the Darling last Sunday.

We did hear, later on, what his real name was; but if we ever chance to read it in the "Missing Friends Column, " we shall not be able to give any information to heart-broken mother or sister or wife, nor to anyone who could let him hear something to his advantage—for we have already forgotten the name.

A TYPICAL BUSH YARN

They were two chaps named Gory and Blanky. They were tramping from Never mineware to Smotherplace. Gory was a bad egg, and Blanky knew it; but they'd fallen in with each other on the track and agreed to travel together for the sake of company. Blanky had £25, which fact was known to Gory, who was stumped.

Every night Gory tried to get the money, which fact was known to Blanky, who never slept with more than one eye shut.

When their tracks divided, Gory said to Blanky:

"Look a-here! Where the deuce do you keep that stuff of yours? I've been tryin' to get holt of it every night when you was asleep. "

"I know you have. " said Blanky.

"Well, where the blazes did you put it? "

"Under your head! "

"The — — you did! "

They grinned, shook hands, and parted; and Gory scratched his head very hard and very often as he tramped along the track.

THE BUSH UNDERTAKER

"Five Bob! "

The old man shaded his eyes and peered through the dazzling glow of that broiling Christmas Day. He stood just within the door of a slab-and-bark hut situated upon the bank of a barren creek; sheep-yards lay to the right, and a low line of bare, brown ridges formed a suitable background to the scene.

"Five Bob! " shouted he again; and a dusty sheep-dog rose wearily from the shaded side of the but and looked inquiringly at his master, who pointed towards some sheep which were straggling from the flock.

"Fetch 'em back, " he said confidently.

The dog went off, and his master returned to the interior of the hut.

"We'll yard 'em early, " he said to himself; "the super won't know. We'll yard 'em early, and have the arternoon to ourselves. "

"We'll get dinner, " he added, glancing at some pots on the fire. "I cud do a bit of doughboy, an' that theer boggabri'll eat like tater-marrer along of the salt meat. " He moved one of the black buckets from the blaze. "I likes to keep it jist on the sizzle, " he said in explanation to himself; "hard bilin' makes it tough—I'll keep it jist a-simmerin'. "

Here his soliloquy was interrupted by the return of the dog.

"All right, Five Bob, " said the hatter, "dinner'll be ready dreckly. Jist keep yer eye on the sheep till I calls yer; keep 'em well rounded up, an' we'll yard 'em afterwards and have a holiday. "

This speech was accompanied by a gesture evidently intelligible, for the dog retired as though he understood English, and the cooking proceeded.

"I'll take a pick an' shovel with me an' root up that old blackfellow, " mused the shepherd, evidently following up a recent train of thought; "I reckon it'll do now. I'll put in the spuds. "

The last sentence referred to the cooking, the first to a blackfellow's grave about which he was curious.

"The sheep's a-campin', " said the soliloquizer, glancing through the door. "So me an' Five Bob'll be able to get our dinner in peace. I wish I had just enough fat to make the pan siss; I'd treat myself to a leather-jacket; but it took three weeks' skimmin' to get enough for them theer doughboys. "

In due time the dinner was dished up; and the old man seated himself on a block, with the lid of a gin-case across his knees for a table. Five Bob squatted opposite with the liveliest interest and appreciation depicted on his intelligent countenance.

Dinner proceeded very quietly, except when the carver paused to ask the dog how some tasty morsel went with him, and Five Bob's tail declared that it went very well indeed.

"Here y'are, try this, " cried the old man, tossing him a large piece of doughboy. A click of Five Bob's jaws and the dough was gone.

"Clean into his liver! " said the old man with a faint smile. He washed up the tinware in the water the duff had been boiled in, and then, with the assistance of the dog, yarded the sheep.

This accomplished, he took a pick and shovel and an old sack, and started out over the ridge, followed, of course, by his four-legged mate. After tramping some three miles he reached a spur, running out from the main ridge. At the extreme end of this, under some gum-trees, was a little mound of earth, barely defined in the grass, and indented in the centre as all blackfellows' graves were.

He set to work to dig it up, and sure enough, in about half an hour he bottomed on payable dirt.

When he had raked up all the bones, he amused himself by putting them together on the grass and by speculating as to whether they had belonged to black or white, male or female. Failing, however, to arrive at any satisfactory conclusion, he dusted them with great care, put them in the bag, and started for home.

He took a short cut this time over the ridge and down a gully which was full of ring-barked trees and long white grass. He had nearly reached its mouth when a great greasy black goanna clambered up a sapling from under his feet and looked fightable.

"Dang the jumpt-up thing! " cried the old man. "It 'gin me a start! "

At the foot of the sapling he espied an object which he at first thought was the blackened carcass of a sheep, but on closer examination discovered to be the body of a man; it lay with its forehead resting on its hands, dried to a mummy by the intense heat of the western summer.

"Me luck's in for the day and no mistake! " said the shepherd, scratching the back of his head, while he took stock of the remains. He picked up a stick and tapped the body on the shoulder; the flesh sounded like leather. He turned it over on its side; it fell flat on its back like a board, and the shrivelled eyes seemed to peer up at him from under the blackened wrists.

He stepped back involuntarily, but, recovering himself, leant on his stick and took in all the ghastly details.

There was nothing in the blackened features to tell aught of name or race, but the dress proclaimed the remains to be those of a European. The old man caught sight of a black bottle in the grass, close beside the corpse. This set him thinking. Presently he knelt down and examined the soles of the dead man's blucher boots, and then, rising with an air of conviction, exclaimed: "Brummy! by gosh! —busted up at last!

"I tole yer so, Brummy, " he said impressively, addressing the corpse. "I allers told yer as how it 'ud be—an' here y'are, you thundering jumpt-up cuss-o'-God fool. Yer cud earn more'n any man in the colony, but yer'd lush it all away. I allers sed as how it 'ud end, an' now yer kin see fur y'self.

"I spect yer was a-comin' t' me t' get fixt up an' set straight agin; then yer was a-goin' to swear off, same as yer 'allers did; an' here y'are, an' now I expect I'll have t' fix yer up for the last time an' make yer decent, for 'twon't do t' leave yer alyin' out here like a dead sheep. "

He picked up the corked bottle and examined it. To his great surprise it was nearly full of rum.

"Well, this gits me, " exclaimed the old man; "me luck's in, this Christmas, an' no mistake. He must 'a' got the jams early in his spree, or he wouldn't be a-making for me with near a bottleful left. Howsomenever, here goes. "

Looking round, his eyes lit up with satisfaction as he saw some bits of bark which had been left by a party of strippers who had been getting bark there for the stations. He picked up two pieces, one about four and the other six feet long, and each about two feet wide, and brought them over to the body. He laid the longest strip by the side of the corpse, which he proceeded to lift on to it.

"Come on, Brummy, " he said, in a softer tone than usual, "ye ain't as bad as yer might be, considerin' as it must be three good months since yer slipped yer wind. I spect it was the rum as preserved yer. It was the death of yer when yer was alive, an' now yer dead, it preserves yer like—like a mummy. "

Then he placed the other strip on top, with the hollow side downwards—thus sandwiching the defunct between the two pieces—removed the saddle-strap, which he wore for a belt, and buckled it round one end, while he tried to think of something with which to tie up the other.

"I can't take any more strips off my shirt, " he said, critically examining the skirts of the old blue overshirt he wore. "I might get a strip or two more off, but it's short enough already. Let's see; how long have I been a-wearin' of that shirt; oh, I remember, I bought it jist two days afore Five Bob was pupped. I can't afford a new shirt jist yet; howsomenever, seein' it's Brummy, I'll jist borrow a couple more strips and sew 'em on agen when I git home. "

He up-ended Brummy, and placing his shoulder against the middle of the lower sheet of bark, lifted the corpse to a horizontal position; then, taking the bag of bones in his hand, he started for home.

"I ain't a-spendin' sech a dull Christmas arter all, " he reflected, as he plodded on; but he had not walked above a hundred yards when he saw a black goanna sidling into the grass.

"That's another of them theer dang things! " he exclaimed. "That's two I've seed this mornin'. "

Presently he remarked: "Yer don't smell none too sweet, Brummy. It must 'a' been jist about the middle of shearin' when yer pegged out. I wonder who got yer last cheque. Shoo! theer's another black goanner—theer must be a flock of 'em. "

He rested Brummy on the ground while he had another pull at the bottle, and, before going on, packed the bag of bones on his shoulder under the body, and he soon stopped again.

"The thunderin' jumpt-up bones is all skew-whift, " he said. "'Ole on, Brummy, an' I'll fix 'em" —and he leaned the dead man against a tree while he settled the bones on his shoulder, and took another pull at the bottle.

About a mile further on he heard a rustling in the grass to the right, and, looking round, saw another goanna gliding off sideways, with its long snaky neck turned towards him.

This puzzled the shepherd considerably, the strangest part of it being that Five Bob wouldn't touch the reptile, but slunk off with his tail down when ordered to "sick 'em. "

"Theer's sothin' comic about them theer goanners, " said the old man at last. "I've seed swarms of grasshoppers an' big mobs of kangaroos, but dang me if ever I seed a flock of black goanners afore!"

On reaching the hut the old man dumped the corpse against the wall, wrong end up, and stood scratching his head while he endeavoured to collect his muddled thoughts; but he had not placed Brummy at the correct angle, and, consequently, that individual fell forward and struck him a violent blow on the shoulder with the iron toes of his blucher boots.

The shock sobered him. He sprang a good yard, instinctively hitching up his moleskins in preparation for flight; but a backward glance revealed to him the true cause of this supposed attack from the rear. Then he lifted the body, stood it on its feet against the chimney, and ruminated as to where he should lodge his mate for the night, not noticing that the shorter sheet of bark had slipped down on the boots and left the face exposed.

"I spect I'll have ter put yer into the chimney-trough for the night, Brummy, " said he, turning round to confront the corpse. "Yer can't expect me to take yer into the hut, though I did it when yer was in a worse state than—Lord! "

The shepherd was not prepared for the awful scrutiny that gleamed on him from those empty sockets; his nerves received a shock, and it was some time before he recovered himself sufficiently to speak.

"Now, look a-here, Brummy, " said he, shaking his finger severely at the delinquent, "I don't want to pick a row with yer; I'd do as much for yer an' more than any other man, an' well yer knows it; but if yer starts playin' any of yer jumpt-up pranktical jokes on me, and a-scarin' of me after a-humpin' of yer 'ome, by the 'oly frost I'll kick yer to jim-rags, so I will. "

This admonition delivered, he hoisted Brummy into the chimney-trough, and with a last glance towards the sheep-yards, he retired to his bunk to have, as he said, a snooze.

He had more than a snooze, however, for when he woke, it was dark, and the bushman's instinct told him it must be nearly nine o'clock.

He lit a slush-lamp and poured the remainder of the rum into a pannikin; but, just as he was about to lift the draught to his lips, he heard a peculiar rustling sound overhead, and put the pot down on the table with a slam that spilled some of the precious liquor.

Five Bob whimpered, and the old shepherd, though used to the weird and dismal, as one living alone in the bush must necessarily be, felt the icy breath of fear at his heart.

He reached hastily for his old shot-gun, and went out to investigate. He walked round the but several times and examined the roof on all sides, but saw nothing. Brummy appeared to be in the same position.

At last, persuading himself that the noise was caused by possums or the wind, the old man went inside, boiled his billy, and, after composing his nerves somewhat with a light supper and a meditative smoke, retired for the night. He was aroused several times before midnight by the same mysterious sound overhead, but, though he rose and examined the roof on each occasion by the light of the rising moon, he discovered nothing.

At last he determined to sit up and watch until daybreak, and for this purpose took up a position on a log a short distance from the hut, with his gun laid in readiness across his knee.

After watching for about an hour, he saw a black object coming over the ridge-pole. He grabbed his gun and fired. The thing disappeared. He ran round to the other side of the hut, and there was a great black goanna in violent convulsions on the ground.

Then the old man saw it all. "The thunderin' jumpt-up thing has been a-havin' o' me, " he exclaimed. "The same cuss-o'-God wretch has a-follered me 'ome, an' has been a-havin' its Christmas dinner off of Brummy, an' a-hauntin' o' me into the bargain, the jumpt-up tinker! "

As there was no one by whom he could send a message to the station, and the old man dared not leave the sheep and go himself, he determined to bury the body the next afternoon, reflecting that the authorities could disinter it for inquest if they pleased.

So he brought the sheep home early and made arrangements for the burial by measuring the outer casing of Brummy and digging a hole according to those dimensions.

"That 'minds me, " he said. "I never rightly knowed Brummy's religion, blest if ever I did. Howsomenever, there's one thing sartin— none o' them theer pianer-fingered parsons is a-goin' ter take the trouble ter travel out inter this God-forgotten part to hold sarvice over him, seein' as how his last cheque's blued. But, as I've got the fun'ral arrangements all in me own hands, I'll do jestice to it, and see that Brummy has a good comfortable buryin'—and more's unpossible. "

"It's time yer turned in, Brum, " he said, lifting the body down.

He carried it to the grave and dropped it into one corner like a post. He arranged the bark so as to cover the face, and, by means of a piece of clothes-line, lowered the body to a horizontal position. Then he threw in an armful of gum-leaves, and then, very reluctantly, took the shovel and dropped in a few shovelfuls of earth.

"An' this is the last of Brummy, " he said, leaning on his spade and looking away over the tops of the ragged gums on the distant range.

This reflection seemed to engender a flood of memories, in which the old man became absorbed. He leaned heavily upon his spade and thought.

"Arter all, " he murmured sadly, "arter all—it were Brummy.

"Brummy, " he said at last. "It's all over now; nothin' matters now—nothin' didn't ever matter, nor—nor don't. You uster say as how it 'ud be all right termorrer" (pause); "termorrer's come, Brummy—come fur you—it ain't come fur me yet, but—it's a-comin'. "

He threw in some more earth.

"Yer don't remember, Brummy, an' mebbe yer don't want to remember—I don't want to remember—but—well, but, yer see that's where yer got the pull on me. "

He shovelled in some more earth and paused again.

The dog rose, with ears erect, and looked anxiously first at his master and then into the grave.

"Theer oughter be somethin' sed, " muttered the old man; "'tain't right to put 'im under like a dog. Theer oughter be some sort o' sarmin. " He sighed heavily in the listening silence that followed this remark and proceeded with his work. He filled the grave to the brim this time, and fashioned the mound carefully with his spade. Once or twice he muttered the words, "I am the rassaraction. " As he laid the tools quietly aside, and stood at the head of the grave, he was evidently trying to remember the something that ought to be said. He removed his hat, placed it carefully on the grass, held his hands

44

out from his sides and a little to the front, drew a long deep breath, and said with a solemnity that greatly disturbed Five Bob: "Hashes ter hashes, dus ter dus, Brummy—an'—an' in hopes of a great an' gerlorious rassaraction! "

He sat down on a log near by, rested his elbows on his knees and passed his hand wearily over his forehead—but only as one who was tired and felt the heat; and presently he rose, took up the tools, and walked back to the hut.

And the sun sank again on the grand Australian bush—the nurse and tutor of eccentric minds, the home of the weird.

THE LEGEND OF COOEE GULLY

The night came down thro' Deadman's Gap,
 Where the ghostly saplings bent
Before a wind that tore the fly
 From many a digger's tent.

Dark as pitch, and the rain rushed past
 On a wind that howled again;
And we crowded into the only hut
 That stood on the hillside then.

The strong pine rafters creaked and strained,
 'Til we thought that the roof would go;
And we felt the box-bark walls bend in
 And bulge like calico.

A flood had come from the gorges round:
 Thro' the gully's bed it poured.
Down many a deep, deserted shaft
 The yellow waters roared.

The scene leapt out when the lightning flashed
 And shone with a ghastly grey;
And the night sprang back to the distant range
 'Neath a sky as bright as day.

Then the darkness closed like a trap that was sprung,
 And the night grew black as coals,
And we heard the ceaseless thunder
 Of the water down the holes.

And now and then like a cannon's note
 That sounds in the battle din,
We heard the louder thunder spring
 From a shaft, when the sides fell in.

We had gathered close to the broad hut fire
 To yarn of the by-gone years,
When a coo-ee that came from the flooded grounds
 Fell sharp on our startled ears.

We sprang to our feet, for well we knew
 That in speed lay the only hope;
One caught and over his shoulder threw
 A coil of yellow rope.

Then, blinded oft by the lightning's flash,
 Down the steep hillside we sped,
And at times we slipped on the sodden path
 That ran to the gully's bed.

And on past many a broken shaft
 All reckless of risk we ran,
For the wind still brought in spiteful gusts
 The cry of the drowning man.

But the cooeying ceased when we reached the place;
 And then, ere a man could think,
We heard the treacherous earth give way
 And fall from a shaft's black brink.

And deep and wide the rotten side
 Slipped into the hungry hole,
And the phosphorus leapt and vanished
 Like the flight of the stranger's soul.

And still in the sound of the rushing rain,
 When the night comes dark and drear,
From the pitch-black side of that gully wide
 The coo-ee you'll hear and hear.

Coo-ee—coo-e-e-e, low and eerily,
 It whispers afar and drear
And then to the heart like an icy dart

It strikes thro' the startled ear!

Dreader than wrung from the human tongue
 It shrieks o'er the sound of the rain,
And back on the hill when the wind is still
 It whispers and dies again.

And on thro' the night like the voice of a sprite
 That tells of a dire mishap
It echoes around in the gully's bound
 And out thro' Deadman's Gap.

MACQUARIE'S MATE

The chaps in the bar of Stiffner's shanty were talking about Macquarie, an absent shearer—who seemed, from their conversation, to be better known than liked by them.

"I ain't seen Macquarie for ever so long, " remarked Box-o'-Tricks, after a pause. "Wonder where he could 'a' got to? "

"Jail, p'r'aps—or hell, " growled Barcoo. "He ain't much loss, any road. "

"My oath, yer right, Barcoo! " interposed "Sally" Thompson. "But, now I come to think of it, Old Awful Example there was a mate of his one time. Bless'd if the old soaker ain't comin' to life again! "

A shaky, rag-and-dirt-covered framework of a big man rose uncertainly from a corner of the room, and, staggering forward, brushed the staring thatch back from his forehead with one hand, reached blindly for the edge of the bar with the other, and drooped heavily.

"Well, Awful Example, " demanded the shanty-keeper. "What's up with you now? "

The drunkard lifted his head and glared wildly round with bloodshot eyes.

"Don't you—don't you talk about him! Drop it, I say! DROP it! "

"What the devil's the matter with you now, anyway? " growled the barman. "Got 'em again? Hey? "

"Don't you—don't you talk about Macquarie! He's a mate of mine! Here! Gimme a drink! "

"Well, what if he is a mate of yours? " sneered Barcoo. "It don't reflec' much credit on you—nor him neither. "

The logic contained in the last three words was unanswerable, and Awful Example was still fairly reasonable, even when rum oozed out of him at every pore. He gripped the edge of the bar with both hands, let his ruined head fall forward until it was on a level with his temporarily rigid arms, and stared blindly at the dirty floor; then he straightened himself up, still keeping his hold on the bar.

"Some of you chaps, " he said huskily; "one of you chaps, in this bar to-day, called Macquarie a scoundrel, and a loafer, and a blackguard, and—and a sneak and a liar. "

"Well, what if we did? " said Barcoo, defiantly. "He's all that, and a cheat into the bargain. And now, what are you going to do about it?"

The old man swung sideways to the bar, rested his elbow on it, and his head on his hand.

"Macquarie wasn't a sneak and he wasn't a liar, " he said, in a quiet, tired tone; "and Macquarie wasn't a cheat! "

"Well, old man, you needn't get your rag out about it, " said Sally Thompson, soothingly. "P'r'aps we was a bit too hard on him; and it isn't altogether right, chaps, considerin' he's not here. But, then, you know, Awful, he might have acted straight to you that was his mate. The meanest blank—if he is a man at all—will do that. "

"Oh, to blazes with the old sot! " shouted Barcoo. "I gave my opinion about Macquarie, and, what's more, I'll stand to it. "

"I've got—I've got a point for the defence, " the old man went on, without heeding the interruptions. "I've got a point or two for the defence. "

"Well, let's have it, " said Stiffner.

"In the first place—in the first place, Macquarie never talked about no man behind his back. "

There was an uneasy movement, and a painful silence. Barcoo reached for his drink and drank slowly; he needed time to think— Box-o'-Tricks studied his boots—Sally Thompson looked out at the weather—the shanty-keeper wiped the top of the bar very hard— and the rest shifted round and "s'posed they'd try a game er cards. "

Barcoo set his glass down very softly, pocketed his hands deeply and defiantly, and said:

"Well, what of that? Macquarie was as strong as a bull, and the greatest bully on the river into the bargain. He could call a man a liar to his face—and smash his face afterwards. And he did it often, too, and with smaller men than himself. "

There was a breath of relief in the bar.

"Do you want to make out that I'm talking about a man behind his back? " continued Barcoo, threateningly, to Awful Example. "You'd best take care, old man. "

"Macquarie wasn't a coward, " remonstrated the drunkard, softly, but in an injured tone.

"What's up with you, anyway? " yelled the publican. "What yer growling at? D'ye want a row? Get out if yer can't be agreeable! "

The boozer swung his back to the bar, hooked himself on by his elbows, and looked vacantly out of the door.

"I've got—another point for the defence, " he muttered. "It's always best—it's always best to keep the last point to—the last. "

"Oh, Lord! Well, out with it! Out with it! "

"Macquarie's dead! That—that's what it is! "

Everyone moved uneasily: Sally Thompson turned the other side to the bar, crossed one leg behind the other, and looked down over his hip at the sole and heel of his elastic-side—the barman rinsed the glasses vigorously—Longbones shuffled and dealt on the top of a cask, and some of the others gathered round him and got interested—Barcoo thought he heard his horse breaking away, and went out to see to it, followed by Box-o'-Tricks and a couple more, who thought that it might be one of their horses.

Someone—a tall, gaunt, determined-looking bushman, with square features and haggard grey eyes—had ridden in unnoticed through the scrub to the back of the shanty and dismounted by the window.

When Barcoo and the others re-entered the bar it soon became evident that Sally Thompson had been thinking, for presently he came to the general rescue as follows:

"There's a blessed lot of tommy-rot about dead people in this world—a lot of damned old-woman nonsense. There's more sympathy wasted over dead and rotten skunks than there is justice done to straight, honest-livin' chaps. I don't b'lieve in this gory sentiment about the dead at the expense of the living. I b'lieve in justice for the livin'—and the dead too, for that matter—but justice for the livin'. Macquarie was a bad egg, and it don't alter the case if he was dead a thousand times. "

There was another breath of relief in the bar, and presently somebody said: "Yer tight, Sally! "

"Good for you, Sally, old man! " cried Box-o'-Tricks, taking it up. "An', besides, I don't b'lieve Macquarie is dead at all. He's always dyin', or being reported dead, and then turnin' up again. Where did you hear about it, Awful? "

The Example ruefully rubbed a corner of his roof with the palm of his hand.

"There's—there's a lot in what you say, Sally Thompson, " he admitted slowly, totally ignoring Box-o'-Tricks. "But—but—'

"Oh, we've had enough of the old fool, " yelled Barcoo. "Macquarie was a spieler, and any man that ud be his mate ain't much better. "

"Here, take a drink and dry up, yer ole hass! " said the man behind the bar, pushing a bottle and glass towards the drunkard. "D'ye want a row? "

The old man took the bottle and glass in his shaking bands and painfully poured out a drink.

"There's a lot in what Sally Thompson says, " he went on, obstinately, "but—but, " he added in a strained tone, "there's another point that I near forgot, and none of you seemed to think of it—not even Sally Thompson nor—nor Box-o'-Tricks there. "

Stiffner turned his back, and Barcoo spat viciously and impatiently.

"Yes, " drivelled the drunkard, "I've got another point for—for the defence—of my mate, Macquarie—"

"Oh, out with it! Spit it out, for God's sake, or you'll bust! " roared Stiffner. "What the blazes is it? "

"HIS MATE'S ALIVE! " yelled the old man. "Macquarie's mate's alive! That's what it is! "

He reeled back from the bar, dashed his glass and hat to the boards, gave his pants, a hitch by the waistband that almost lifted him off his feet, and tore at his shirt-sleeves.

"Make a ring, boys, " he shouted. "His mate's alive! Put up your hands, Barcoo! By God, his mate's alive! "

Someone had turned his horse loose at the rear and had been standing by the back door for the last five minutes. Now he slipped quietly in.

"Keep the old fool off, or he'll get hurt, " snarled Barcoo.

Stiffner jumped the counter. There were loud, hurried words of remonstrance, then some stump-splitting oaths and a scuffle, consequent upon an attempt to chuck the old man out. Then a crash. Stiffner and Box-o'-Tricks were down, two others were holding Barcoo back, and someone had pinned Awful Example by the shoulders from behind.

"Let me go! " he yelled, too blind with passion to notice the movements of surprise among the men before him. "Let me go! I'll smash—any man—that—that says a word again' a mate of mine behind his back. Barcoo, I'll have your blood! Let me go! I'll, I'll, I'll—Who's holdin' me? You—you—-"

"It's Macquarie, old mate! " said a quiet voice.

Barcoo thought he heard his horse again, and went out in a hurry. Perhaps he thought that the horse would get impatient and break loose if he left it any longer, for he jumped into the saddle and rode off.

THE MYSTERY OF DAVE REGAN

"And then there was Dave Regan, " said the traveller. "Dave used to die oftener than any other bushman I knew. He was always being reported dead and turnin' up again. He seemed to like it—except once, when his brother drew his money and drank it all to drown his grief at what he called Dave's 'untimely end'. Well, Dave went up to Queensland once with cattle, and was away three years and reported dead, as usual. He was drowned in the Bogan this time while tryin' to swim his horse acrost a flood—and his sweetheart hurried up and got spliced to a worse man before Dave got back.

"Well, one day I was out in the bush lookin' for timber, when the biggest storm ever knowed in that place come on. There was hail in it, too, as big as bullets, and if I hadn't got behind a stump and crouched down in time I'd have been riddled like a—like a bushranger. As it was, I got soakin' wet. The storm was over in a few minutes, the water run off down the gullies, and the sun come out and the scrub steamed—and stunk like a new pair of moleskin trousers. I went on along the track, and presently I seen a long, lanky chap get on to a long, lanky horse and ride out of a bush yard at the edge of a clearin'. I knowed it was Dave d'reckly I set eyes on him.

"Dave used to ride a tall, holler-backed thoroughbred with a body and limbs like a kangaroo dog, and it would circle around you and sidle away as if it was frightened you was goin' to jab a knife into it.

"''Ello! Dave! ' said I, as he came spurrin' up. 'How are yer! '

"''Ello, Jim! ' says he. 'How are you? '

"''All right! ' says I. 'How are yer gettin' on? '

"But, before we could say any more, that horse shied away and broke off through the scrub to the right. I waited, because I knowed Dave would come back again if I waited long enough; and in about ten minutes he came sidlin' in from the scrub to the left.

"'Oh, I'm all right, ' says he, spurrin' up sideways; 'How are you? '

"'Right! ' says I. 'How's the old people? '

"'Oh, I ain't been home yet, ' says he, holdin' out his hand; but, afore I could grip it, the cussed horse sidled off to the south end of the clearin' and broke away again through the scrub.

"I heard Dave swearin' about the country for twenty minutes or so, and then he came spurrin' and cursin' in from the other end of the clearin'.

"'Where have you been all this time? ' I said, as the horse came curvin' up like a boomerang.

"'Gulf country, ' said Dave.

"'That was a storm, Dave, ' said I.

"'My oath! ' says Dave.

"'Get caught in it? '

"'Yes. '

"'Got to shelter? '

"'No. '

"'But you're as dry's a bone, Dave! '

"Dave grinned. '— —and— —and— —the— — —! ' he yelled.

"He said that to the horse as it boomeranged off again and broke away through the scrub. I waited; but he didn't come back, and I reckoned he'd got so far away before he could pull up that he didn't think it worth while comin' back; so I went on. By-and-bye I got thinkin'. Dave was as dry as a bone, and I knowed that he hadn't had time to get to shelter, for there wasn't a shed within twelve miles. He wasn't only dry, but his coat was creased and dusty too — same as if he'd been sleepin' in a holler log; and when I come to think of it, his face seemed thinner and whiter than it used ter, and so did his hands and wrists, which always stuck a long way out of his coat-sleeves; and there was blood on his face — but I thought he'd got scratched with a twig. (Dave used to wear a coat three or four sizes too small for him, with sleeves that didn't come much below his elbows and a tail that scarcely reached his waist behind.) And his hair seemed dark and lank, instead of bein' sandy and stickin' out like an old fibre brush, as it used ter. And then I thought his voice sounded different, too. And, when I enquired next day, there was no one heard of Dave, and the chaps reckoned I must have been drunk, or seen his ghost.

"It didn't seem all right at all — it worried me a lot. I couldn't make out how Dave kept dry; and the horse and saddle and saddle-cloth was wet. I told the chaps how he talked to me and what he said, and how he swore at the horse; but they only said it was Dave's ghost and nobody else's. I told 'em about him bein' dry as a bone after gettin' caught in that storm; but they only laughed and said it was a dry place where Dave went to. I talked and argued about it until the chaps began to tap their foreheads and wink — then I left off talking. But I didn't leave off thinkin' — I always hated a mystery. Even Dave's father told me that Dave couldn't be alive or else his ghost wouldn't be round — he said he knew Dave better than that. One or two fellers did turn up afterwards that had seen Dave about the time that I did — and then the chaps said they was sure that Dave was dead.

"But one fine day, as a lot of us chaps was playin' pitch and toss at the shanty, one of the fellers yelled out:

"'By Gee! Here comes Dave Regan! '

"And I looked up and saw Dave himself, sidlin' out of a cloud of dust on a long lanky horse. He rode into the stockyard, got down, hung his horse up to a post, put up the rails, and then come slopin' towards us with a half-acre grin on his face. Dave had long, thin bow-legs, and when he was on the ground he moved as if he was on roller skates.

""'El-lo, Dave! ' says I. 'How are yer? '

""'Ello, Jim! ' said he. 'How the blazes are you? '

"''All right! ' says I, shakin' hands. 'How are yer? '

"''Oh! I'm all right! ' he says. 'How are yer poppin' up! '

"Well, when we'd got all that settled, and the other chaps had asked how he was, he said: 'Ah, well! Let's have a drink. '

"And all the other chaps crawfished up and flung themselves round the corner and sidled into the bar after Dave. We had a lot of talk, and he told us that he'd been down before, but had gone away without seein' any of us, except me, because he'd suddenly heard of a mob of cattle at a station two hundred miles away; and after a while I took him aside and said:

"''Look here, Dave! Do you remember the day I met you after the storm? '

"He scratched his head.

"''Why, yes, ' he says.

"''Did you get under shelter that day? '

"''Why—no. '

"''Then how the blazes didn't yer get wet? '

"Dave grinned; then he says:

"'Why, when I seen the storm coming I took off me clothes and stuck 'em in a holler log till the rain was over. '

"'Yes, ' he says, after the other coves had done laughin', but before I'd done thinking; 'I kept my clothes dry and got a good refreshin' shower-bath into the bargain. '

"Then he scratched the back of his neck with his little finger, and dropped his jaw, and thought a bit; then he rubbed the top of his head and his shoulder, reflective-like, and then he said:

"'But I didn't reckon for them there blanky hailstones. '"

A DERRY ON A COVE

'Twas in the felon's dock he stood, his eyes were black and blue;
His voice with grief was broken, and his nose was broken, too;
He muttered, as that broken nose he wiped upon his cap—
'It's orfal when the p'leece has got a derry on a chap.

'I am a honest workin' cove, as any bloke can see,
'It's just because the p'leece has got a derry, sir, on me;
'Oh, yes, the legal gents can grin, I say it ain't no joke—
'It's cruel when the p'leece has got a derry on a bloke.'

'Why don't you go to work?' he said (he muttered, 'Why don't you?').
'Yer honer knows as well as me there ain't no work to do.
'And when I try to find a job I'm shaddered by a trap—
'It's awful when the p'leece has got a derry on a chap.'

I sigh'd and shed a tearlet for that noble nature marred,
But, ah! the Bench was rough on him, and gave him six months' hard.
He only said, 'Beyond the grave you'll cop it hot, by Jove!
'There ain't no angel p'leece to get a derry on a cove.'

TROUBLE ON THE SELECTION

You lazy boy, you're here at last,
    You must be wooden-legged;
Now, are you sure the gate is fast
    And all the sliprails pegged
And all the milkers at the yard,
    The calves all in the pen?
We don't want Poley's calf to suck
    His mother dry again.

And did you mend the broken rail
    And make it firm and neat?
I s'pose you want that brindle steer
    All night among the wheat.
And if he finds the lucerne patch,
    He'll stuff his belly full;
He'll eat till he gets 'blown' on that
    And busts like Ryan's bull.

Old Spot is lost? You'll drive me mad,
    You will, upon my soul!
She might be in the boggy swamps
    Or down a digger's hole.
You needn't talk, you never looked
    You'd find her if you'd choose,
Instead of poking 'possum logs
    And hunting kangaroos.

How came your boots as wet as muck?
    You tried to drown the ants!
Why don't you take your bluchers off,
    Good Lord, he's tore his pants!
Your father's coming home to-night;
    You'll catch it hot, you'll see.
Now go and wash your filthy face
    And come and get your tea.

Printed in the United Kingdom by
Lightning Source UK Ltd., Milton Keynes
139227UK00003B/77/P